D1514908

SAM and the SILVER STONES

Copyright © 2008 by AequiLibris Publishing, LLC
All rights reserved.

No part of this book may be reproduced, stored in a retrieval system, or transmitted, in any form or by any means—electronic, mechanical, photocopying, or otherwise—without prior written permission from the publisher.

ISBN 978-0-9816446-1-5 (hardcover)
Library of Congress Control Number: 2008905929

Text type set in 15 point Garamond.
Book design by Judy Arisman, arismandesign.com
Printed in Canada by Dollco Printing

© Mixed Sources
Product group from well-managed forests, controlled sources and recycled wood or fiber
www.fsc.org Cert no. SW-COC-001506
© 1996 Forest Stewardship Council
FSC

Printed with vegetable-based ink.

AequiLibris Publishing, LLC
59 Fieldstone Lane
PO Box 1542
New London, New Hampshire 03257
603.526.4187
www.AequiLibrisPublishing.com

SAM and the
SILVER
STONES

By Mary Kuechenmeister
and Brinker Ferguson

Illustrated by Rushyan Yen

AequiLibris LLC

Every morning when I wake up, I ask myself the same question:
What amazing things are going to happen today?

Chapter *One*

I don't mean to make you nervous or anything, but the story you're about to read is true. It happened to me—well, to us, really, the kids in my class—and no one has been the same since. It's all because of Sal. We met him at the city art museum when we were there for a field trip. I suppose you could call Sal a tour guide—but he's not exactly what you'd call a typical tour guide.

Oh, by the way, my name is Sam. Sam Richardson. Samuel Augustus Richardson, to be exact, but no one calls me that except my mom, and that's only when she's mad.

A little while ago my best friend, Alec, started calling me by my initials, S.A. I didn't mind at first, but the other kids thought he was calling me Essay, like when you write a paper for class, and now they're all calling me that. Essay Richardson. I guess the kids figure Essay is a good nickname because I like to write.

Before all of this happened with Sal, things weren't exactly going my way. There were less than two weeks left in the school year and I had to write a huge paper on something that had special meaning to me.

I was thinking of writing about the day we got our dog Jake, or when my little sister Joanne was born. But I was only two when both things happened, and it's not like I was real clear on the details.

A girl in my class was supposed to draw pictures to go along with my story, but she came down with chicken pox. So I was on my own—not only to write the paper, but to make the illustrations for it too.

On top of that, the dentist told my mom I needed braces. Braces! Great way to start the summer.

Add to that a trip to the art museum when—at that point—I would rather have been anywhere else and, let me tell you, I was a kid in need of a serious vacation.

It was already hot at 9:15 in the morning when the school bus dropped us off in front of the museum. Six of us had signed up for the trip: Alec, Emily, Roger, Buddy, Erin, and me.

Well, I didn't exactly sign up, as you may have already figured out. It's more like I *ended up.* If I hadn't been late to school the morning everyone was choosing field trips, I would have made the cutoff for the water park trip instead.

But there I was at the museum with Ms. Burke, standing in the roasting sun and thinking about all the kids in the wave pool while I listened to her go over the rules.

"No running. No loud talking. Stay with the group. And above all," she said, "don't touch the artwork! Do you understand?" When no one answered, she said it again. "Do you understand?"

We all answered at the same time. "Yes, Ms. Burke."

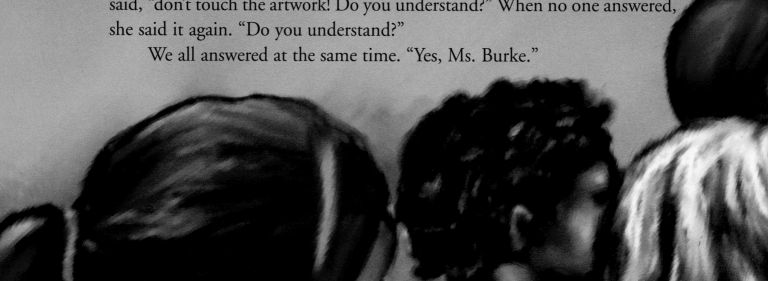

"Very good. Now, I just want to make sure everyone is here."
There were only six of us.

"Alec?" she called out.

He rolled his eyes.

"Alec?" she repeated.

"I'm right here," he said.

"Just raise your hand and say 'present.'"

"Present and accounted for, Ms. Burke. May I leave now?"

"No, you may not, and don't be a wise guy, Alec." She looked up from her clipboard. "And take off your hat when we go inside."

"But I'll have hat head," he protested.

"Are you chewing gum?" she asked.

He smiled and blew a giant pink bubble. "Yep."

"Get rid of it," she told him. "Roger?"

"Here, Ms. Burke. I mean *present*."

Roger's quiet. Real quiet. He blushes when you look at him, but he's the best darn drummer Westwood Regional ever had. Put a set of drumsticks in Roger's hands and even the school band rocks.

"Emily?"

"Yes, Ms. Burke. I'm here."

I think Emily is the only one who actually wanted to come to the museum. She loves art. She's pretty good at it, too. Last summer she drew a picture of Jake. It's amazing—it looks just like him.

"Sam?" Ms. Burke continued.

"That would be you, Essay." I guess Alec just wanted to make sure I was clear on that.

I raised my hand. "That would be me," I agreed. "Present."

A small bead of sweat ran down Ms. Burke's forehead. "Okay, Buddy and Erin, you two are here. Come on. Let's get inside where it's cool."

We walked through a large stone arch into the lobby of the museum. The place was huge and crawling with people. There were school groups like ours, and mothers with kids in strollers, and people from all over the world walking around and talking to each other in languages I couldn't understand.

She'd arranged for our group to have a "special guided tour." I don't think she had a clue at that point just how special.

The weird thing was, everyone seemed so excited to be there. Ms. Burke called us over to a spot at the foot of a giant marble stairway that, she explained, led upstairs to the galleries.

That's where we'd be spending the morning, she said. She'd arranged for our group to have a "special guided tour." I don't think she had a clue at that point just how special.

6

Chapter *Two*

No sooner did she mention this than a man appeared right next to her, out of nowhere. Ms. Burke was so surprised that she stumbled backward and almost fell onto the stairs.

"Oh, my!" she gasped. "You're here."

"At your service," the man replied with a bow.

"Whoa!" Alec said admiringly.

"Where'd he come from?" I asked Buddy. But Bud just stood there, gaping.

The guide was wearing a beret, a black and white striped shirt, pants that were too short, and bright red high-top sneakers. And his eyes—they sparkled with this incredible silver light.

"Get a load of that guy," Alec whispered.

Of course it was loud enough that everyone could hear. We all cracked up.

"Class!" Ms. Burke gave us one of her killer looks. "You're the guide, then?" You could tell Ms. Burke was a little freaked.

He nodded. "Sal's the name. So pleased to make your acquaintance," he said. Then he abruptly turned away, as if something else had caught his attention. "Excuse me," he said to Ms. Burke. "Did you hear that?"

"Pardon?" she asked. "Hear what?"

Just then, a voice called out over the loudspeaker, "MS. JULIA BURKE. MS. JULIA BURKE. PLEASE COME TO THE INFORMATION CENTER IMMEDIATELY."

"Oh, my! Why do you suppose they want me?" she asked in wonder. She reached behind her for her purse, and when she did her glasses fell from her face onto the floor.

She bent down to pick them up and the entire contents of her purse—pennies, buttons, safety pins, wallet, keys, lipstick, pens, mints—spilled all over the place. "Oh, I don't know what's wrong with me," she said. "Sal," she called to him over her shoulder. "Can you help me, please?"

When he bent down to help her pick up her things, she waved him away impatiently. "No, no," she said. "The kids. Help me with the kids. This is Sam, Erin, Alec, Buddy, Emily, Roger." She introduced us in one long breath. "Would you mind taking them on ahead? I'll catch up with you. I should only be a minute. Where will you be? What gallery?"

"MS. JULIA BURKE." It was the voice over the loudspeaker again.

"Oh, my." Without waiting for Sal to answer, Ms. Burke stood, smoothed the wrinkles from her skirt, and ran off in the direction of the information counter.

"Ms. Burke. Ms. Burke!" Alec called after her, but she didn't hear. "I'm going to wear my hat inside. You don't mind, do you?"

"Okay, Sam, Erin, Alec, Buddy, Emily, Roger, let's get started," said Sal, repeating our names in the exact order Ms. Burke had introduced us. "Walk this way."

With that, Sal spun around in a circle, took two giant steps forward, and leapt high in the air! Then he turned, took a deep bow from the waist, and looked up, waiting for the rest of us to follow. "Come along," he urged. "Nothing to it."

Roger, who was closest to him, stood like he was bolted to the floor. "Um," he said.

10

"We're not playing freeze tag, Rog. Go on, man, do it," Alec called out, laughing. But Roger didn't move.

Sal nodded to Emily. "How about you?" he asked.

"Do I have to?"

Sal shook his head. "There's nothing that you have to do," he said. "Today is about you. Do what you want to do. Like everything in life, my friends, you will get from today what you put into it, and the same for tomorrow and the next day and the day after that. But always remember, there's much to be gained when you're open to new experiences."

No one was willing to give it a shot. Not even Alec.

It was my turn. "Oh, what the heck,"

I said. I mean, really, how much worse could my week get? I stepped forward, spun in a circle, took two giant steps, and leapt into the air. It was amazingly fun.

"Very good, my boy." For the second time that morning I saw the quick flash of silver in his eyes. "Today is about discovery," Sal said to the class. "So, like your friend Sam here, keep yourself open to new experiences and you'll be amazed by what you will learn."

Alec punched me lightly on the shoulder. I smiled and shrugged.

We followed Sal up the stairs and through a maze of rooms until he finally stopped in gallery number twenty-seven. I wondered how Ms. Burke was ever going to find us. Seems to me most people probably

Photo: Jorge P. Anders.
Photo credit: Bildarchiv Preussischer Kulturbesitz/Art Resource
Gemäldegalerie, Staatliche Museum zu Berlin, Berlin, Germany

Brueghel, Pieter the Elder (c.1525-1569). *The Netherlandish Proverbs.*
1559. Oil on oak panel, 117 x 163 cm. Inv. 1720.

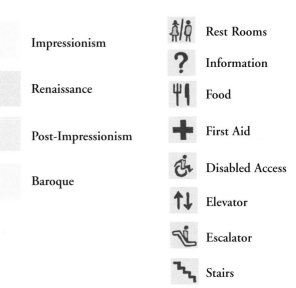

■ Impressionism	🚻 Rest Rooms
■ Renaissance	? Information
■ Post-Impressionism	🍴 Food
■ Baroque	✚ First Aid
	♿ Disabled Access
	↑↓ Elevator
	Escalator
	Stairs

Digital Image © The Museum of Modern Art
Licensed by SCALA/Art Resource, NY
The Museum of Modern Art, New York, NY, U.S.A.

Rousseau, Henri (1844-1910) Le Douanier.
The Sleeping Gypsy. 1897. Oil on canvas, 51" x 6' 7".
Gift of Mrs. Simon Guggenheim. (649.1939)

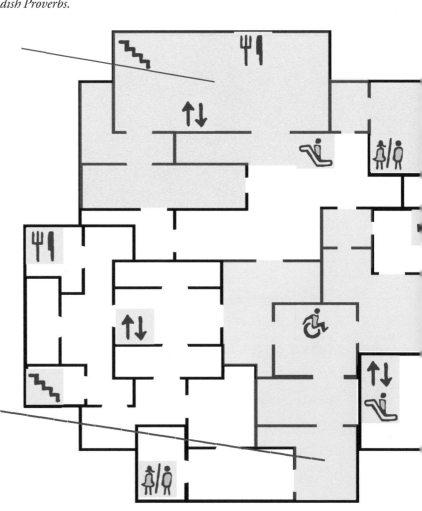

City Art

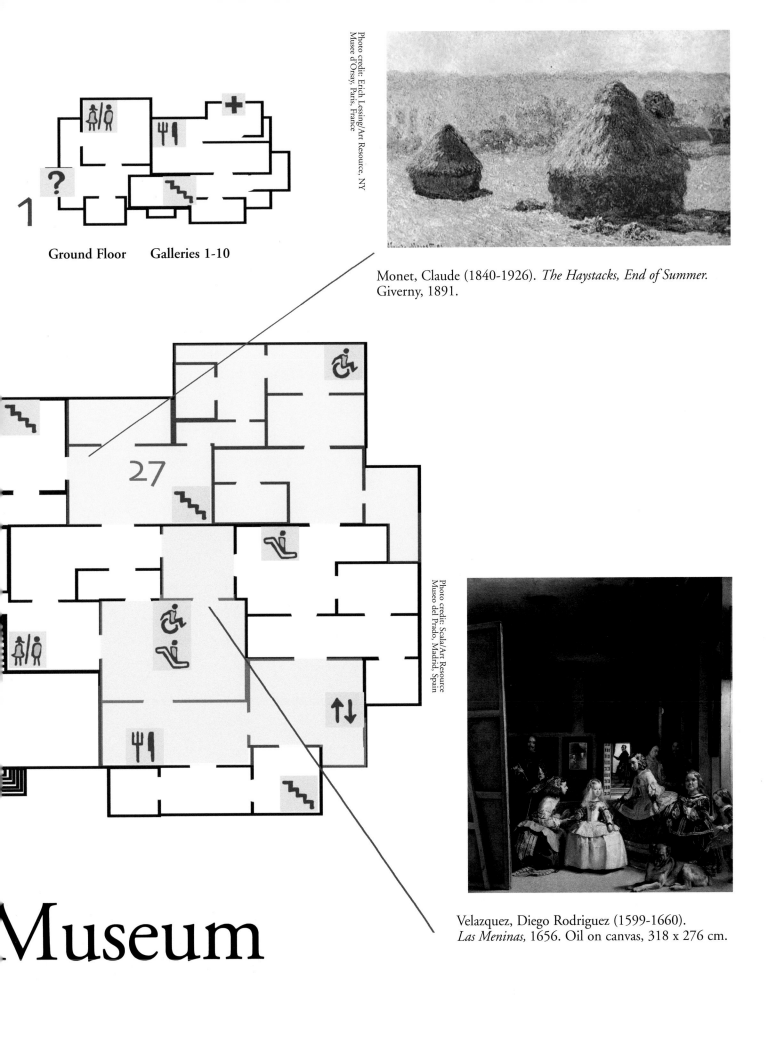

Photo credit: Erich Lessing/Art Resource, NY
Musée d'Orsay, Paris, France

Ground Floor   Galleries 1-10

Monet, Claude (1840-1926). *The Haystacks, End of Summer.*
Giverny, 1891.

Photo credit: Scala/Art Resource
Museo del Prado, Madrid, Spain

Velazquez, Diego Rodriguez (1599-1660).
Las Meninas, 1656. Oil on canvas, 318 x 276 cm.

Museum

started in gallery number one and made their way to—oh, I don't know—gallery number two, maybe. Not Sal, apparently. He started in the middle.

"Ah, yes. Here they are." Sal walked directly over to a wall that had four pictures of haystacks hanging on it. "Monet," he said. "Claude Monet. A Frenchman, you know. The granddaddy of *Impressionism.*"

"Is he talking to us?" Alec asked. "In English?"

14

"That's the name of the artist," Emily told Alec. "Claude Monet. The paintings that he's looking at are part of the haystack series."

"Good to know, Em. Thanks. Essay, you taking notes?"

"Okay, everyone, over here." Sal lined us up shoulder to shoulder about ten feet from the paintings. "Every picture tells a story, my friends, about its subject and its artist. Let's start with an easy question, though: What do you see?"

15

Chapter *Three*

"Haystacks." Roger answered so quietly that it was hard to hear.

"Very good!" Sal told him. "All of you, take one giant step forward. Now what do you see?"

Buddy raised his hand. "Haystacks," he said proudly.

"Oh, brother. It's going to be a long day," Alec said.

"Okay," Sal said. "Move forward again. Alec, it's your turn. Tell me what you see."

"Hay . . ." he started to say, but he caught himself. "Wait a minute. Actually, I just see little dabs of paint."

"Ah!" Sal's eyes sparkled with delight. "Now, go back to where you started." We all stepped back and the haystacks appeared again.

"Now," he said to us, "this time I want you to look a little harder. What do you *really* see?" Everyone was quiet for a moment. Then Alec raised his hand again.

"Haystacks," he said, blowing another of his giant pink bubbles.

"Anyone else?" Sal asked.

"I see color," Emily said.

"I see the exact same haystack in all four paintings, but in different colors," Buddy added.

"Sam, how about you?" Sal asked. "Tell me what you see." Wacky as he was, there was something about the guy I was beginning to like. He made me feel like I could say whatever I wanted and it would be okay.

"I see light," I told him. Alec smirked.

"Go on."

"Sunlight and shadow. I see warmth and cold." Now Alec was squinting at the paintings suspiciously.

17

"Could it be I hear the voice of a poet?" Sal remarked. He put his hand on my shoulder. "Move in closer, please." Sal and I stood in front of the haystack painting that he told me was called *End of Summer, Morning*.

From behind us Alec joked, "Hey, Sal, is there one called *End of Day* so we could go home?"

Turning around, he said to Alec, "*End of Day* is here too, my friend. Be patient." Then he turned back again. "You see all the brilliant colors Monet used?" he said. "That's how he captured light. Up close, it's hard to make sense of, but if you stand back you can see the haystack and you know it's morning. In that one, you see how it looked at midday. Over there, it's *End of Day*, of course. Alec's favorite! When you look at a Monet, it's all about the light."

I'm an official, you know, an official official. Would you care to see my badge?

Just then a lady with red hair and a museum badge poked her head into the gallery and gave us all the once-over. "Stand back from the art," she scolded. "Not too close."

"Thank you, madame." Sal was all smiles. "Job well done. Yes, of course, not too close. No cause for alarm. I'm an official, you know, an *official* official. Would you care to see my badge?" he asked.

He pointed to the front of his shirt, but of course there was no badge, not even a nametag. Her eyes narrowed as she backed out of the room. I wondered if she was going to get security.

"Just doing her job," Sal said to us solemnly. Then he brightened. "Now, all of you, sit on the floor in front of these paintings. There are things to learn. What is it I say? Keep your mind open and your eyes wide. Remember that, would you? In case I forget."

He smiled and turned back to the paintings.

"Monet was one of the first artists to try to paint *exactly* what he saw. Doesn't sound like much to us now, but it was revolutionary at the time, and not very well liked, I should add. At first, very few people understood what he was doing. Critics called him an *Impressionist*, and they were not being kind. They thought his work looked unfinished, like it was only the impression of something, and the name stuck.

"But he was like a scientist, really. Monet observed nature incredibly closely, breaking light down the way a prism does. And he used different kinds of brushstrokes and *lots* of layers of paint. You're looking at four of his paintings that are, basically, about light.

"He often worked from dawn to dusk on his haystacks, sometimes swapping one canvas for another as the sun made its way across the sky. He painted haystacks in different weather, and in different seasons. You see how he was able to capture the light's effect on the haystack's color and texture? Aside from the fact that it's beautiful, his work is also insanely cool. Agreed?"

"Agreed," we answered in unison.

Sal nodded, pleased. "Now, who wants to go on a treasure hunt?" We all raised our hands. "Good show! We'll be looking at four different paintings," he went on, "including Monet's *End of Summer, Morning*. There is a clue in each—and at the end, a surprise!"

It sounded easy enough. Sal stood for a moment looking at us, then said, "I choose the poet who doesn't yet know it. Samuel, please step forward.

"Last time I counted," he continued, "there were 652,175 paintings and art objects in this museum. And you know what? They all have one thing in common. In fact, all of the art in the entire world and all of the artists who ever made anything have this one thing in common. Do you know what it is?"

I shook my head.

"Do you want to find out?"

I nodded, even though I wasn't sure what I was getting myself into.

"Okay," he said. "Say goodbye to your friends and step over here." Say goodbye to my friends? I don't know what kind of look I had on my face, but I don't think it was good.

He put his hand on my shoulder and turned me so that I was directly facing *End of Summer, Morning*.

"Close your eyes, Sam. Ready?" he asked.

Before I could answer, I started to twirl. Suddenly my entire body was caught in the spin cycle of some wild whirligig!

"Stop!" I tried to yell, but there was no sound. "Sal! Help me!" I strained to get the words out.

20

I don't know how long it went on: a second, a minute, an hour? Everything was a blur. Then it stopped, and there I was: sitting on top of a . . . a haystack. No, really. And not just any haystack. *Monet's* haystack.

"Sam!" From somewhere way off in the distance, I heard Emily's voice.

"Em? Is that you? Where are you?" I put my hand over my eyes so I could see better. The light was intense. "Emily?"

"Pretty bright in there, huh? Should have brought your shades." It was Sal. "You might want to climb down and find your first clue. This could take a while, after all."

I could see Sal then, and the others too. Their faces were inches from the painting, and they were huge.

Sal winked at my friends. "He's looking a little flushed," he said. "Is it me, or is anyone else picking up shades of vermillion?"

"Hey, Sal," I called out. "I don't want to play this game. Get me out of here, would you?" I wondered what the heck *vermillion* was.

"No problem. All you need to do is find the clues."

"I don't want to find the clues. I want out now. And what's vermillion?"

"Afraid it doesn't *"Oh, and Sam, be a good lad and stay where I can see you. Can't get you back otherwise."* work that way," he shrugged. "Sometimes I wish it did, but no. Once you're in, you're in to the end. Didn't I mention that earlier? So many things to remember. Oh, and vermillion is a reddish-orange color. One of Monet's favorites.

"Oh, and Sam, be a good lad and stay where I can see you. Can't get you back otherwise."

"Is there anything else I need to know?" I think my voice cracked.

"Not that I can think of at the moment. Let's move along. Don't have all day."

Have you ever tried to get down off the top of a haystack? It's not exactly easy. Let's just say I fell. Well, crash-landed is actually more like it. And backwards, not forwards.

Chapter *Four*

It gets worse. It's just white canvas back there. It's not like Monet painted the ground *behind* the haystack. And once I was back there, there was no way out. That paint dries hard.

"Essay!" I could hear Alec. "We can't see you, man. Not funny."

"Sam!" Emily and Erin's voices blended together. Then they were all shouting my name.

I don't want to say I panicked, but I didn't know what to do.

"Sal!" I called his name over and over and banged on the wall of paint, but it was no use.

To make matters worse, it occurred to me that even if I found the clue, I might not recognize it. Sal had forgotten to tell me what I was looking for. A map, a flower, a pin, a flag? I had no idea.

"Sal!" I called out again. No answer. What were they going to tell my parents? *Lost in a painting, Mr. and Mrs. Richardson. So sorry. Monet's haystack, you know. Yes, a lovely work of art.*

I sat down and let my head drop into my hands.

"Think, Sam, think," I said aloud.

If I was able to fall *out* of the painting, couldn't I fall back *in*? Well, at least it was a plan.

I had come down head first, so I tried something crazy: I did a handstand in the exact same spot where I had landed.

I wiggled my feet in the air to find a hole, or wrinkle, or whatever it was

I had fallen through. At first I didn't feel a thing, but then my right foot sank into something like quicksand. Then my left foot sank.

I was getting sort of woozy from being upside-down so long, but I heard what sounded like a muffled roar. It was my friends—they could see my feet and were cheering me on. It must have looked pretty crazy.

But this was, Sal reminded the class, a Monet. What did they expect?

Okay, what next? I kicked my legs around until the hole got big enough to back through. Then, just as I found the haystack again I did a somersault down the front of it and landed flat on my backside. Everybody cheered.

When I sat up, I saw that I was covered in the craziest colors under the sun. Red and blue and yellow and green bits of hay were stuck to my clothes and my hair. Then I realized it wasn't hay at all, but *paint*.

I guess I must have looked kind of funny, because there was a lot of laughing. But this was, Sal reminded the class, a Monet. What did they expect?

He turned back to me, looking relieved.

"Your shoe is untied," he said.

I reached down to tie it and that's when I saw what had to be the first clue. It was a silver stone, small enough to fit into the center of my hand, and etched into it were the letters C and R.

"Okay, Sal, here it is." I held up the stone for him. "Are we done now?"

"No, my friend. There are three more paintings to see, and three more clues to find. Come along, there's much to discover."

"Where am I going now?"

I have to admit, I was curious.

"You'll see."

Oh boy.

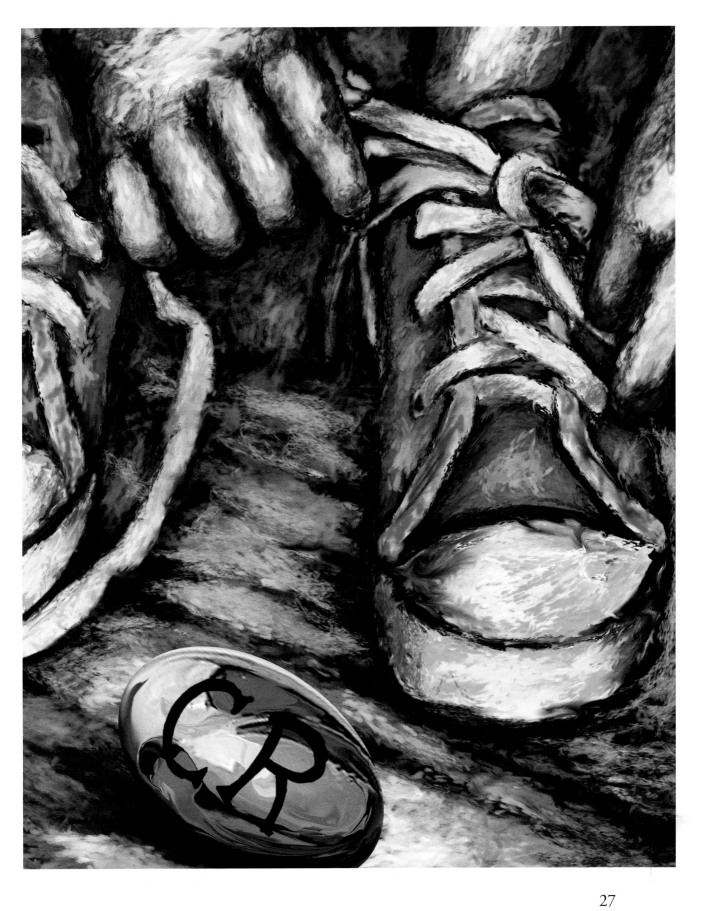

Sal put me back in the spin cycle. It's a good thing I'm not the carsick type. Everything was a giant blur, and when I landed, I wished it had stayed that way. I was on a rooftop in some sort of crazy village. There were people all over the place doing the weirdest things.

"Friends of yours, Sal?" I asked.

No answer. That's when I realized that, aside from all the nuts in the picture, I was completely alone.

"Hello?" I called out. "Anybody home?"

That's when the fellow next to me, the one with the toothache who was hanging a picture of a crescent moon out the window, looked over his shoulder at me and said, "I think he's over there."

The man pointed to a guy who was—best as I could tell—banging his head against a brick wall.

"Yeah, great, thanks," I said. "By the way, where am I? And who are all these people?"

But he had already turned away.

As I was looking around some more, I heard a voice. "Stay together, please. Everybody with me."

It was Sal—he was somewhere close, making his way through the maze of rooms to find me.

"Sam!" I heard Alec call out. "Come out, come out, wherever you are."

"In here," I hollered. "This way!"

No one in the village paid any attention to me. I could have yodeled at the top of my lungs or sung a round of "John Jacob Jingleheimer Schmidt." It wouldn't have mattered. I sat down and pulled sticks of hay out of my hair. What a day. Then I looked at the stone.

"C R," I said to myself. "Stands for crazy."

"Hello?" I shouted again, not even bothering to lift my head.

"Hello!" a woman's voice called back. "Who's there?"

No way! I thought at first maybe I was seeing things, but, sure enough, there she was—the lady with the red hair. She was in the gallery, not ten feet away from me.

"I insist that you step forward and identify yourself immediately," she demanded.

I barely allowed myself to breathe as I watched her search. She bent down to look under the viewing benches and then went over to the windows. She karate-chopped the curtains.

"I know someone's in here," she said. "You can't hide from me."

I closed my eyes and listened to the heavy clomping of her shoes as she circled the room. At last she left and the sound faded away to nothing.

"Oh, Sal," I said under my breath. "Where are you?"

Chapter *Five*

Alec and Emily entered the gallery ahead of everyone else.

"I can hear you, but I can't see you," Alec said. "Am I getting warm? Come out, come out, wherever you are. Wave your hands. Jump up and down—anything!"

"Guys! I'm here!" I stood up and, without thinking, did what Alec suggested: I jumped.

I quickly discovered that it's not a good idea to jump on a rooftop. I completely lost my footing and fell to the ground. I landed just about on top of a man who was absorbed in tying a bell to a cat's collar. Even more strangely, he was wearing a full suit of armor.

I smiled at him and brushed the dirt off my pant leg. "I guess that's a dangerous job. It's good to see you're taking every precaution."

He ignored me as I hurried past.

"Hey!" I yelled out to Alec. "Do you see me now?" I jumped up and down next to the man who was hitting his head on the wall. "Still at it?" I asked him. "Care for an aspirin?"

No response. I don't think they were too keen on me.

"Whoa, Essay, there you are!" Alec and Emily finally saw me as I rounded another corner.

"Sam! This is so cool. Do you know where you are?" Emily asked me. "You're in a Brueghel painting. It's called *Netherlandish Proverbs*. It's from the 1500s. Boy, did you ever go back in time."

"That makes you what—five hundred years old, Essay?" Alec's eyes widened. "You're looking pretty good, man."

Best to ignore Alec at the moment, I decided, and direct my questions to Emily. After all, the girl knew her stuff.

"Was everybody crazy back then?" I asked her.

"No," she answered, "Brueghel was a storyteller. This painting's full of proverbs—little lessons about life, you know? Just look around you—there's a guy throwing money down the drain back there." She laughed. "And there's a lady crying over spilled milk."

Just then Sal came rushing in, with the rest of the class following along behind.

"Samuel, my boy, good to see you," he said, with a huge smile. "And right where I hoped you'd be!" He turned to the class.

"Our friend here is in a painting by Pieter Brueghel. Quite the scene, don't you agree?"

"Sam and I know that already," Alec informed him. "Emily told us."

"Oh!" Sal sounded pleased. "Well then, for the rest of you, a little background. Pieter Brueghel was born in Belgium in about 1525, and he's considered to be one of the greatest painters of his time. A large part of what makes Brueghel's work great is that he created a style all his own. He didn't paint what was expected of him, and he didn't paint in a way that was popular at the time. Instead, Brueghel painted the way he wanted and showed life as he saw it. Imagine that, a free thinker—his *creativity* made him stand apart."

"Hey, Sal? Remember me?" I shouted. "I hate to be a pest, but can you help me out here? Like maybe tell me what I'm supposed to do?"

"Why, find the clue, my boy, of course."

"But there are a million different places it could be," I protested.

"Probably more than a million," Alec piped up.

"Do you think?" Sal asked.

"I'd say two million. Maybe even three." Alec wasn't going to give it up.

"Hey, do you mind?" I yelled out.

"Be patient, Samuel, and listen to me. You'll find this interesting. Now where was I? Ah, yes, creativity!

"Back in Brueghel's day, artists liked to paint portraits, either of rich and powerful people or of religious figures. Hardly anyone painted poor, country people—peasants, as they were called. Except for Brueghel, that is. In fact, he was so interested in the lives of common people that he used to dress up like a peasant and take trips into the countryside.

"He'd mosey around in villages just to observe the people. He painted scenes of everyday folks going about their business. Sometimes he'd sneak into weddings and celebrations and mix with the crowd. If you look closely, you'll see that his paintings are very detailed, and they teach us a lot about what life was like back then.

Because of this, many people thought Brueghel was a peasant himself, but he wasn't. He was actually quite well-to-do.

"He drew people in a realistic, three-dimensional way. That was something that they had just learned how to do back then. He also liked to tell stories with his paintings and they often include hidden messages, like we see in our little friend's painting, here."

"Our little friend?" I asked. Boy, the guy knew how to push my buttons.

"Come to think of it, you *are* only about half an inch tall, Sam," Alec laughed. "It works for me."

The others started to laugh too, but I gave them a firm look that stopped them.

Sal kept on. "Brueghel painted images of over one hundred different proverbs in this painting. A lot of the proverbs are no longer used, so they don't mean much to us anymore." Sal studied the painting for a moment. "Do you see this fellow here?" he asked the class.

I walked out to the center of the painting, so I could see too.

Sal pointed to a man who was fishing. "Do you see what he's doing?" he asked. "He's fishing behind a net. Hey!" Sal called out to him. "Bad spot. You're not going to catch anything there."

"Can he hear you?" I asked.

It hadn't occurred to me that maybe the people in the painting could see and hear Sal too.

"No. Just thought I'd try anyway. A heads-up, you know. Poor fellow. Complete waste of time. Five hundred years and not a single bite. You see, to 'fish behind the net' means to do something in such a way that you miss all opportunity.

"And here," he pointed again. "Do you see this old woman?" Now I really had to crane my neck. "The proverb is 'fear makes gallop the old woman.' We don't use that one anymore, but, well, you get the point.

"Anyway, enough," Sal announced. "We could stay here all day and figure out these proverbs, but," he cupped his hand over his mouth, "*our little friend . . .*" he whispered.

"Hey, I heard that!" Boy, that burned me.

"Oh, yes, of course. I forgot. But the point is, Samuel, you need to get going. We don't have all day, you know."

I was so peeved—the guy was lucky I was only half an inch tall.

I don't know why, but I made my way over to the lady crying over the spilled milk.

"Excuse me, ma'am," I started to say, but when she looked up at me, I jumped.

She was holding something between her teeth—something large and *silver*.

"Hey!" I cried out to my friends. "Either that's the stone in her mouth, or she's got a whopper of a filling there."

I couldn't believe my luck. I moved closer and, sure enough, the woman had the stone clenched between her teeth as she sobbed.

I needed her to stop crying, so I thought about what someone might say to me if I were upset. You know, how they'd be really gentle with their words. I crouched down so I could look her right in the eye and said, "Don't you know, ma'am, that there's no sense crying over spilled milk?"

Chapter *Six*

It didn't work. In fact, I think I made it worse. "Oh, for goodness sake!" I said to no one special. I didn't know what to do. "Anybody have a tissue?" I threw up my hands.

"I know!" It was Alec. "Tell her a joke. Give her a good laugh. Maybe the stone will fall out."

"Your friend knows the power of laughter, Sam. That's his gift," Sal told me. "Listen to him."

"Say something funny about milk," Alec went on. "Try this one: *If a cow laughed, would milk come out her nose?* She'll love it!"

So, for the second time in Brueghel's painting, I did what Alec suggested. I bent down and said to the lady, "Hey lady, ever hear the one about the cow?" And then I told her the joke.

Like magic, she stopped crying, and I saw a small smile cross her lips. Then she started to laugh. She laughed so hard that the stone fell out of her mouth and landed in the puddle of milk. I reached out and grabbed it. She didn't seem to notice.

I stood up and wiped it clean on my shirt. Brueghel's stone was just like Monet's, only the letters I V I T were etched into the center.

"I've got it, Sal," I yelled, holding both stones up for him to see. "CRIVIT. Is that right? Or VICTIR? Victory, maybe?"

"You're getting there, my boy," Sal said. "But you've got more to discover yet."

Somehow I knew he was going to say that.

"Hold on."

Next thing I knew I'd been whirled into my next painting. By now I was getting pretty used to it. Only this time I landed hard, face down on the ground. I stayed there for a few minutes with my eyes closed until I stopped spinning.

Was that sand against my cheek? Ah! I thought, the beach. Sal's decided to give me a break this time. But when I opened my eyes and picked up my head, there was no rolling surf, no seagull gliding lazily by. Not even close. I was in a desert and face-to-face with a lion!

"What, have you lost your mind, Sal? How could you do this to me?" I stood up and slowly, very slowly, backed away and looked out into the gallery. This time the class was already there, all of them. I got the feeling they'd been waiting for me.

"You know there's a law against this kind of stuff, Sal," I told him. "You can't just whirl people into pictures with man-eating lions!" I was hopping mad.

"I don't think he's hungry, Essay," Alec volunteered. "I've been watching him and he's just minding his own business."

"Well, that's a relief!" I said. Now I was mad at Alec too. I was mad at all of them. "Anyone else have any genius things to say?"

"Samuel, please, relax for a moment and listen. When you know more, you'll feel better."

"What, another lesson on how to catch fish?" I couldn't help myself, but when he didn't respond, I did what he said: I sat down and listened. What else could I do?

"This painting is called *The Sleeping Gypsy*," Sal said. "It's by Henri Rousseau. Like Monet, Rousseau was French, and also like Monet, Rousseau's work was generally not liked when he first started painting. People laughed at Rousseau and called his work ridiculous and childlike because it appears so flat on the canvas. But over time people came to appreciate those qualities. They're part of what makes a Rousseau painting so special.

"Everything Rousseau knew about art, he learned on his own. He came from a poor family and never attended art school or took an art lesson. He taught himself to paint by studying the works of masters at art museums.

And he painted one color at a time, working from the top of the canvas to the bottom. His paintings appear flat partly because of that, and also because he never had a teacher who taught him about dimension and depth.

"So many different things to see when you look at art," Sal responded. "It's interesting that Roger focuses on the music."

So Rousseau developed his own style—sound familiar? And today he is considered one of the world's greatest artists.

"Do you know what Rousseau did when people made fun of him? He ignored them. Do you know why? Because he believed in himself. Sometimes it's not easy being different. I bet some of you feel that way. That there are times when it's easier to be just like everyone else. If someone laughs at what you're doing, it makes you want to quit."

"I felt that way when I first started playing the drums," Roger said quietly. The others nodded in understanding.

"Well, imagine if Monet or Brueghel or Rousseau allowed that to happen. The reason they're so great is because they had the courage to be themselves and create, regardless of what other people said. And that, my friends, is not to be forgotten."

"Hey!" I jumped up. "Remember me?" Enough was enough. I guess I moved too quickly, because the lion looked up and eyed me. I swear he licked his chops. "Nice kitty," I said. I sat down again fast. "You want to wrap it up here, Sal?" I whispered.

"Okay, okay," he answered. "But you really should know that Rousseau painted quite a lot of exotic pictures like *The Sleeping Gypsy*, but he never set foot outside of France. Everything he painted in his jungle scenes he saw in museums or gardens, on postcards, or in books. He had an incredible imagination. Sometimes he even frightened himself with what he painted." Sal paused.

"Okay, so what do you think Rousseau was thinking when he painted *The Sleeping Gypsy*? There's no right answer, but let's see if we can help Sam find his clue! Anyone?"

He waited.

"I've got it, Sam! Rousseau was thinking that you should tickle the lion's tootsies and make him laugh," Alec joked.

"Funny, Alec," I answered. "All I know is, if the clue is in the lion's mouth, I give up."

"It's sort of interesting that there's a mandolin in the painting," Roger said slowly, pointing at the instrument.

"So many different things to see when you look at art," Sal responded. "It's interesting that Roger focuses on the music. Go on."

"Well, I'm thinking that maybe mandolin music helped the gypsy get to sleep. So maybe music will put the lion to sleep too. That way Sam could find the next clue without having to worry about being eaten."

"Good thinking," I agreed.

"So who's going to make the music?" Sal asked.

"We are," Roger replied, and the next thing you know, he had the class singing "The Lion Sleeps Tonight." Even Sal jumped in with the chorus.

Sure enough, the lion started to get drowsy. He dropped down onto his side and let out a big yawn. What a relief.

But then, right after he drifted off to sleep, guess who came screaming into the gallery? The lady with the red hair!

"I should have known!" she said to Sal. "It's you again, making a racket and disturbing the peace and quiet!" Then she said to the kids, "You stay right here. I'm going to get help."

And that's when she saw me. Her jaw just about dropped to the ground, and she started spitting and sputtering, but no words came out. She began to back out of the room. Sal walked with her.

"No sudden moves, mister," she warned.

"Really, madame, I think you're quite overreacting," he replied calmly.

But I saw it happen. Before they got to the door, he reached over and touched her on the shoulder, the same as he had done with me.

Next thing I knew, she was in the spin cycle, coming right toward me.

"No!" I shouted.

Chapter *Seven*

But there she was, running down the hill in the background of the painting.

"You're in big trouble, mister," she was hollering. "Don't think people won't miss me. They'll come looking, and when they do . . . " Then she started in on me. "Keep your hands in your pockets. Don't touch this painting, young man."

It didn't seem worth it to remind her that she was right smack in the middle of it already.

Remember that cool singing that put the lion to sleep? Let's just say it wore off. He was awake, and, if you ask me, he looked pretty mad.

"Why put her in here with me, Sal?" I yelled out into the gallery.

"What else could I do?" he answered. "If she alerted others and they hauled me out of here, what then? How could I get you back? We're all safe for the time being. But get on with it, please. Find the clue, Sam."

"I'm the one who wanted to call it quits, remember?"

"Stick with the music, Sam," Roger said. "There has to be a reason why Rousseau put a mandolin in the painting."

The lady was still at it. "Don't make things worse, young man," she was yelling. "Sit quietly and wait for the authorities."

I grabbed the mandolin anyway and strummed a few chords. The lion stared at me.

"Roger!" I called out for help.

"Just keep playing," he answered. "Anything!"

The lion was starting to get up.

"*In the village, the peaceful village, the lion sleeps tonight,*" I croaked.

My hoarse singing was pathetic. The lion crouched, like he was getting ready to pounce.

"Put that thing down," the lady shouted.

But I just strummed the mandolin like a madman.

Then, all of a sudden, there it was. The stone. It must have been lodged in the neck of the instrument. It fell into my hand. I just had a second to look before the lion let out a ferocious roar. The stone had the letters T E A.

"TEA CRIVIT," I yelled. "I think they're cookies."

The lion sprang into the air.

"Now get us out of here!"

With not a second to spare, the spinner started up again.

Only this time, guess who came along for the ride? The lady. If you ask me, I would have been better off with the lion.

Sal had said four paintings. So this was it, the last one. But they were getting crazier by the second. And this time I had company. The lady was a little green around the gills from the ride, but that didn't keep her mouth from working.

"Be quiet," I whispered firmly, but she kept yakking about how much trouble we were all going to be in when this was over.

Once again Sal had put me, well, us, into a painting with people, only this time they didn't look wacky like the others had. In fact, they looked pretty serious. I didn't exactly want to be the one to explain what we were doing there.

Oh, and did I mention the dog? The big dog, with the big teeth? Well, he was there too. Thanks, Sal.

"Where are we?" I called out as quietly as possible.

"Quiet." Sal sounded serious. "Don't talk, just listen. They can't hear me. They can hear only you and . . . what is your name, madame?" he asked.

"Martha," she answered.

Surprisingly, this time she kept her voice low.

"As I was saying, they can hear only you and Martha. And you don't want to be found, Samuel. Trust me on this.

"Everyone," he told the class, "sit."

All the kids dropped to the floor around the painting and waited for Sal to begin. Even Martha buttoned it up to listen.

"This painting is called *Las Meninas,* which is Spanish for *The Maids of Honor.* It was painted in 1656 by a man named Diego Velázquez, and it is one of the most important works of art ever produced. There are powerful people in this painting.

"Velázquez was the official painter in the court of King Philip IV of Spain. He painted portraits of the king and members of his royal family for almost forty years. You're on the backside of Velázquez's canvas now, Sam.

"If you move forward very carefully and look into the room, the little girl in the center with the blonde hair and white dress is the king's daughter, Princess Margarita. The man holding the paintbrush and palette is Velázquez himself. The fact that he's in his own painting is part of what makes this work of art so special.

"For centuries the question has been asked: is Velázquez painting Princess Margarita or is he painting himself? That would be quite bold of him, wouldn't it? Or is it a portrait of the king and queen? If you look up at the wall, you can see them reflected in the mirror.

"*The Maids of Honor* was very different for the time in which it was painted. In that way, Velázquez is like the other artists we've seen today. He took risks. He didn't do what other people expected of him. He trusted himself.

"And what about this: if we could see his canvas, would we discover that we are in the painting too? After all, whomever Velázquez was painting would have been standing right here.

"The others in the room," Sal went on quietly, "are members of the court and handmaids to the princess. The dog, of course, is the family pet. Good-sized, too," he added admiringly, winking at the class.

While I scowled at him, Martha elbowed me. "Okay, one question. Who is he?" she whispered, pointing at Sal.

"He's the tour guide. From the museum," I told her.

She shook her head. "No way. Not that fellow."

"What do you mean?" I asked.

"I've been with the museum for fifteen years and I've never laid eyes on him before today," she told me.

Chapter *Eight*

I felt a chill go up my spine. How could she not know who Sal was if he was a museum tour guide? I started wondering who the heck Sal really was.

"Sal's a good guy," I protested. "Just listen to him and he'll get us out of here. Actually," I explained, "I'm looking for a stone. Like these." I pulled the three stones from my pocket. "They're clues. Once we discover what it is that Sal wants us to learn, he'll bring us back."

She studied the stones in my hand: C R I V I T   T E A.

"You looking for a word?" she asked. I nodded. "Well then, it's easy, isn't it?"

"What do you mean?"

"CRATIVITE," she said. "It's that stuff that makes Superman sick."

"You mean kryptonite?" I asked.

"That's what I just said." She looked at me, obviously quite pleased with herself.

"Yeah, great. Thanks," I said to her. "I don't know why I didn't think of that." What else was there to say? Martha wasn't so bad after all.

"Sam, would you please be quiet!" Sal's voice jarred me. "Remember," he said, "if the king sees you and takes you out of the picture, I won't be able to get you back. I told you that before. Martha, the same goes for you. Do you understand?" he asked her.

"Yes," she answered.

Sal paused for a moment.

"Is that all you're going to say?" I asked him. We couldn't stay hidden behind the canvas for the rest of our lives.

"Thinking, thinking," he responded. "Maybe that dropcloth on the floor would hide you while you look around."

I got down on my hands and knees and peeked around the corner. Sure enough, there was a cloth on the floor to protect it from any paint that dripped from Velázquez's brush.

I tried to grab the cloth, but it was anchored under the canvas. I don't know what Sal was thinking. Of course they saw me.

"Remember," he said, "if the king sees you and takes you out of the picture, I won't be able to get you back."

The dog was the first to jump to his feet, and the princess screamed. That brought the king and queen bustling over. And Velázquez actually dropped his brush.

No one in the room seemed too pleased about seeing us there. They all started to talk at once—in Spanish, of course. And the kids in the gallery had jumped to their feet and started yelling instructions at us too. It was a giant mess.

And then, to top it off, I saw Ms. Burke come into the gallery. It's impossible to describe the look on her face as she tried to figure out what was going on.

The king summoned his guards, or that's what it sounded like. Anyway, two huge men came into the painting and grabbed Martha. She fainted in their arms. There was such a mad scramble to get the princess out of the room that—at least for a short while—they seemed to forget all about me.

"Would someone please tell me what's going on here?" Ms. Burke screeched.

No one was paying attention to her, though.

"Now, Sam! Find the clue!" Sal ordered.

But how, I wondered.

"Look where the princess was standing. She was at the center of the painting. It must be somewhere close to her," Buddy yelled out.

"I say it's on Velázquez's palette," Emily said. "Look there, Sam."

The guards carried Martha up the back stairs and out of the painting.

"Don't fish behind the net, man!" Of course it was Alec. "Try the dog's mouth," he suggested. "There's some sort of dental work thing connected to all of this."

Suddenly I heard Sal's voice above all the others. "Look on the canvas," he told me. "That's always been the big mystery about this painting—what's on Velázquez's canvas. Look fast, Sam. Before the guards come to get you. Oh, and Sam," he added, a bit more quietly.

"Maybe later you'll let me know what you see?"

I tried to make my way to the front of the canvas but more guards came into the room, and this time they were after me.

I started to run, but my foot got tangled in the dropcloth and I fell.

As I was getting up, a small black shoe in the center of the room caught my eye. It was so highly polished that it gleamed in the sunlight. It was clear that it belonged to the princess. When they picked her up, it must have fallen off her foot.

And there, like a buckle on the shoe, was the stone! I grabbed it just as two guards lifted me off my feet. I didn't even have a chance to see what was etched onto the surface.

"Let me go!" I roared as I struggled to break free.

Suddenly everything in the room came to a complete standstill.

"Way to go, Essay!" Alec shouted.

Without taking his eyes from mine, the king walked toward me. No one made a sound. The king nodded to the guards to release me and began to speak. Of course, I couldn't understand him.

"Sal?" I called out under my breath. "I could use a little help here, please. I hope you speak Spanish."

"He's asking who you are. He wants to see what you have in your hand."

"And the answer is?"

"Move very slowly and remove all the stones from your pocket. Hold all four of them together in the palm of your hand and show them to him."

I did as Sal said. The king stepped forward and examined each of the stones closely. They didn't appear to make any kind of impression on him. It's not like I was stealing the royal jewels or anything.

When he turned the last of the four stones over, I saw the letter Y. When the king seemed satisfied that I was not a thief, I slipped them back into my pocket.

CRIVIT Y TEA. CREAT Y VITI. I ran different combinations of letters in my head, desperately trying to find the one word that would get Martha and me out of there.

Martha! A feeling of dread washed over me. I couldn't leave without her.

Chapter *Nine*

All of a sudden there was a commotion on the back stairs. It was Martha. She came flying into the room, with one of the guards just steps behind. Then she turned and tried a karate chop on him. I think I saw him roll his eyes. He threw his arms up in the air and said something to the king in Spanish.

"Sal?" I asked.

"He said he gives up. He can't take anymore."

With that the guard turned and left the room. Martha came over to where I was standing.

"Well, I guess I showed him," she beamed. "Need some help here, Sammy?"

The king just stared at us.

I pulled the stones out of my pocket and showed them to her.

"I found the last one," I explained. "Quick, tell me what you see," I asked.

But then, like it had been there the whole time, I knew the answer.

"CREATIVITY!" I shouted. "That's the word, Sal. It's what all of the artists have in common! CREATIVITY."

With that, light flooded the room and the stones joined into one big stone in the palm of my hand, with the word CREATIVITY plainly etched into it.

The royal family gasped and stepped back in shock. I managed a quick peek out into the gallery and saw my friends actually doing a victory dance. Alec was in the lead, holding on to Ms. Burke's hand. I have to say, she looked a little dazed.

Martha and I stood together, our eyes fixed on the shining stone.

61

Then, through all the confusion, I heard Sal say, "Brilliant, my lad. Well played. Come home now, would you?"

And in no time at all Martha and I were standing on the gallery floor.

We were instant celebrities—well, that's how it felt anyway. Everyone ran over to us. There were hugs and kisses and pats on the back. Alec crowned me *King of the World* and placed his hat on my head as a crown.

Sal watched from a distance. He was smiling, but there was a funny look on his face too, like he was no longer part of what was going on.

"Sal," I called out, but he either didn't hear me or pretended not to. I went over to him.

"It was a great day, Sal," I told him. "Thank you." I held the stone out to him. "You should take it," I said. "It belongs to you."

"You know, Samuel," he said, "the stone has no value. The only creativity that matters is inside you. The stone is just a reminder." He motioned in the direction of the others. "Take a look at your friends. They didn't find the stone, and yet . . ."

I turned to look and, once again, in a day full of remarkable discoveries, I saw something I had never seen before: sparks of silver shining in the eyes of all of the people in the room. It was the same silver as the stone, and—I now realized—the same spark that I had seen in Sal's eyes earlier in the day.

"It's inside them?" I asked.

"It's in all of us," he answered. "It's just a matter of recognizing it."

"I don't think you're a regular guide here, are you, Sal?" I asked. "Martha tells me she's never seen you before."

But before he answered, Ms. Burke's voice filled the gallery. "Okay, class, time to wrap this up!" She had her clipboard back in her hands and appeared fully recovered. "It's been a, well, an *interesting* day. Everybody in line."

"Why did you choose those artists, Sal? And why those paintings?"

There was so much I wanted to know, but even as I started to speak, I realized he was gone. I raised the stone into the air in tribute. I could feel a catch in my throat.

With that, I stepped forward, spun in a circle, took two giant steps, and leapt in the air. Then I took my place in line.

Hey, remember that paper I was having so much trouble with? Well, guess what – you just finished reading it. Emily did the illustrations. Next week Alec, Emily, and I are going back to the museum to find Sal. I want to write another story and Alec wants to be the guy who gets put in all the paintings. That's okay with me. I've had enough excitement – at least for now.

Photo: Ron Pownall

Mary Kuechenmeister, coauthor, has been writing for as long as she can remember. In addition to working as the principal copywriter for an advertising and marketing firm that she headed, she has contributed stories and articles to numerous regional magazines and publications. *Sam and the Silver Stones* is Mary's first children's book. She hopes to continue the series, teaching children about art and art-related themes in a fun and offbeat manner. She graduated from the University of Connecticut at Storrs and resides in New London, New Hampshire. In addition to her work as a writer, Mary volunteers her time to several non-profit organizations, including the Womens Trust, a microfinance organization headquartered in Wilmot, New Hampshire. She is the mother of two adult children. *Sam and the Silver Stones* coauthor Brinker Ferguson is her daughter.

Photo: Ron Pownall

Brinker Ferguson, coauthor, graduated magna cum laude from Wheaton College in Norton, Massachusetts, in 2008 with a degree in art history. She has worked in numerous museums, including the Metropolitan Museum of Art in New York City; the Museum of Fine Arts, de Young, in San Francisco; the Museum of Applied Art, in Vienna; the Trust for Museum Exhibitions in Washington, D.C.; and the Cornish Colony Museum in Windsor, Vermont. Over the past four years she has taught art history appreciation at several elementary schools personifying the character of Sal. She is currently working with Art Refuge/Friends of Tibetan Women's Association, a non-profit organization helping Tibetan children living in northern India to paint, play, and tell their stories through art. Her future plans include travel to New Zealand and India, where she will further her studies before returning to the states to attend graduate school.

Rushyan Yen, illustrator, graduated magna cum laude from Wheaton College in Norton, Massachusetts, in 2008 with a degree in fine arts. While at Wheaton she was awarded the prestigious MARIA VICTORIA DELUCA FORSYTHE PRIZE IN STUDIO ART. As an intern at both the Cholomandal Artist Village in Chennai, India, and the Art and Design Research Center for the 2008 Olympic Games in Beijing, she worked with prominent artists from both countries. Her studies have taken her to Cortona, Italy, where she participated in the University of Georgia Study Abroad Program, and Florence, where she was enrolled at Student Art Center International. She has also taken courses at the Rhode Island School of Design. Chosen as a 2008 Thomas J. Watson Fellow, Rushyan plans to expand her artistic repertoire in nine countries within the course of her fellowship year.

Just when you thought it was safe to bring your kitten to Argentina—Sal's back. This time as a gaucho—that's a South American cowboy—exploring cave painting in Patagonia!!

Watch for
Another Great Sal Adventure:
Rory and the Cave of the Hands,
due out soon.